When Za'atar Met Zeit

By Wafa Shami

Illustrated by Shaima Farouki

ISBN 978-0-9600147-4-3
       0-9600147-4-8

@copywrite 2021 Wafa Shami
Children Fiction Books, Multi-Cultural

Illustrations by Shaima Farouki

October, 2021
Design & Printing Gate Advertising

Printed in the United States of America
U.S. $9.99

To Faris...

Yasmina was a little girl who lived in the hills of Palestine...
She looked out her window one morning and thought
about how she wanted to make her family happy. She was
a great cook, and knew just what she wanted to make!

Za'atar lived up on the small little hills. He was an herb named thyme who is nurtured from the sun warming his little face and the winter rain nourishing his body. He looked so green and happy, and he was excited to be picked and turned into the very tasty herb used on many yummy dishes.

Nearby, Zeituna stood on her hundred year-old tree along with her fellow olives. The little olives were young and starting to bloom, and hope to grow and get stronger to be picked and turned into zeit. Zeit, or oil, comes from olives. Once picked from a tree, the olives are pressed and their juice is called zeit zeitun or olive oil.

One day, Za'atar heard the birds whispering and dancing and talking about an extraordinary aroma coming from the little house up in one of those hills. Za'atar heard his name mentioned along with someone else called Zeit. Za'atar was curious.

"Who is Zeit? I want to meet her," he thought.

He heard the birds whisper of a love story that happens only when Za'atar meets Zeit. It was something out of this world, and made tummies everywhere dance with excitement.

The door to the house opened, and Yasmina came strolling out. She picked Za'atar and took him home. Then Za'atar got a good wash and was laid down on a long white sheet to dry under the warm spring sun. The next day his color started to turn into lighter green.

After he was fully dried he was taken to the grinder. Za'atar was afraid but Yasmina reassured him that the machine would not harm him. After he was ground za'atar was mixed with yummy roasted sesame, deep red sumac, and some other spices, and became colorful and shiny. His smell filled the air with a lovely aroma.

However, he was still feeling a bit lonely, so he decided to keep looking for Zeit so he could see for himself whether that love story the bird told him about would happen.

Zeitouna was picked as well. Soon, she was full of energy, slippery, oily, and just coming out of the olive press. She had turned into Zeit. Excited, she looked around and found herself in a bottle sitting at the kitchen table.

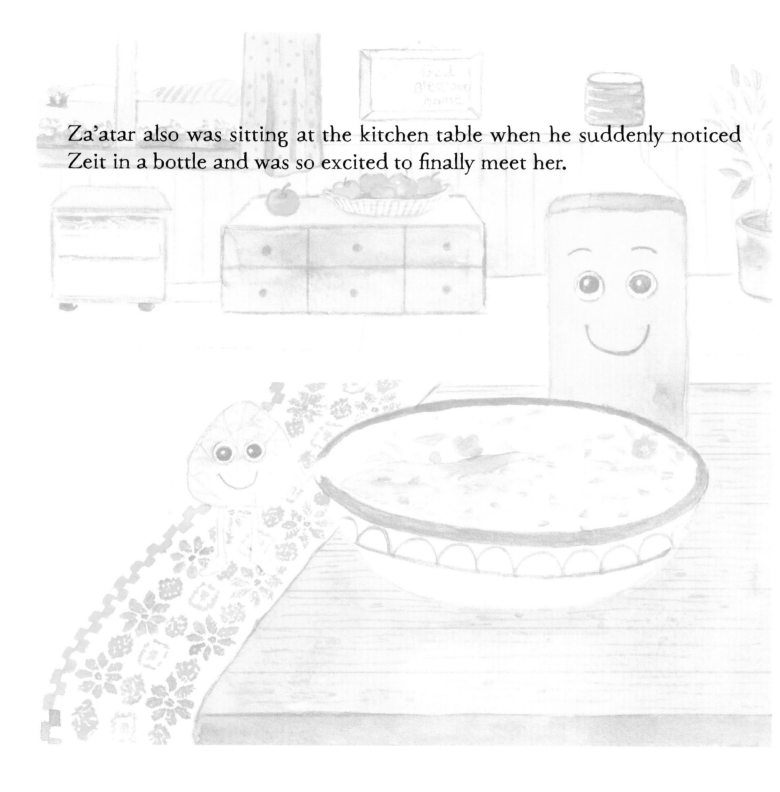

Za'atar also was sitting at the kitchen table when he suddenly noticed Zeit in a bottle and was so excited to finally meet her.

They both realized how much they had in common.
They were both green; they both grew inland. They were
strong, independent plants who could fully take care of
themselves, growing under the sun and being nurtured by
the winter rain.

Za'atar exclaimed that he looked like a little rounded heart.
And Zeit said, "Me too! I'm originally from
a Zeitouna that is more of an oval shape and looks like a real
heart."

They both giggled.

Zeit wi Za'atar were happy together and excited to see what Yasmina would do. They were amazed that Yasmina had a plan to turn them into something tasty!

She worked and worked and worked.

She started making a simple flatbread dough. She poured water over the flour, added yeast, then mixed everything together and kneaded the dough. Once the dough rested and was ready to work with, she cut it into small pieces and rolled each piece into a flat rounded shape.

Next, she mixed Zeit and Za'atar together, and last she poured them over the dough. They went into the oven, and out they came!

And just like that, they turned into man'oushah!
Now Yasmina's house was buzzing. Everyone was gathered around the table, excited to eat, laugh, and
gather together!

Zeit wi Za'atar were so happy to be spread on a man'oushah, filled with love and happiness.

The End

Wafa Shami was born and raised in Ramallah, Palestine. She moved to the U.S. to pursue higher education and graduated with a Master's degree in International Studies. Since moving to the U.S. Wafa has maintained her engagement in Middle Eastern issues as a volunteer. After her son was born she was inspired to write children's storybooks based on her childhood memories Her stories, Easter in Ramallah, and Olive Harvest in Palestine were published in the last few years. Besides being busy raising her son. Wafa who lives in California has a passion for cooking and writes a food blog, in which she shares her family's recipes. Visit her blog at www.palestineinadish.com and follow her on social media @palestineinadish for delicious recipes.

Shaima Farouki is a Palestinian artist born in Jerusalem in 1988. A graduate of Friends School, she currently lives in Ramallah. Shaima has a Bachelor's degree from Birzeit University in Journalism and Social Sciences. She has a passion for, and deep interest in arts and developed her talent through practice and by attending workshops to improve her drawing skills. She has participated in many group art exhibits in Ramallah. Shaima currently creates and sells her paintings and teaches drawing classes. She also works on illustrations for children's storybooks.

Mana'eesh

For Mana'eesh recipe visit the link below:
https://palestineinadish.com/recipes/manæesh-zaatar

Printed in Great Britain
by Amazon

38643531R00021